Building a
community
of readers

Book-Rich Environments Initiative

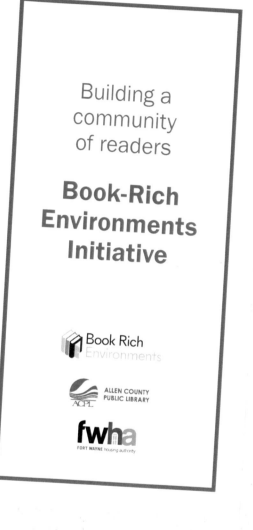

Book Rich
Environments

ALLEN COUNTY
PUBLIC LIBRARY
ACPL

fwha
FORT WAYNE *housing authority*

To Peter, with love ~
JB
To Nina, with love ~
RB

First published in Great Britain in 2011 by Scholastic Children's Books,
a division of Scholastic Ltd

ISBN 978-0-545-93156-4

12 11 10 9 8 7 6 5 4 3 2 1   15 16 17 18 19 20/0

Printed in the U.S.A.   40

This edition first printing, November 2015

Little Deer Lost

Written by
Janet Bingham

Illustrated by
Rosalind Beardshaw

SCHOLASTIC INC.

Silver and Sparkle were racing
through the woods.
"I'm winning!" called Silver.

Suddenly, he stopped.
Sparkle bumped into him –

thump!

"Look!" gasped Silver.
Shimmering white flakes were drifting
down from the sky.
One landed on Sparkle's nose. "It's cold!"
she giggled in surprise.

Silver caught one on his tongue
and felt it melt. "It's wet, too," he said.
"I think it's snow!" cried Sparkle,
dancing with excitement.
"It's beautiful, just like Mommy said,
and it's…"
"…fun!" added Silver. "Let's play!"

Soon the sky was full of snowflakes.
Silver chased them, and Sparkle
flicked them with her tail.
As the snow settled, Silver kicked
up little flurries, and Sparkle made
patterns with her footprints.

After a while the snowflakes stopped falling, and Silver and Sparkle gazed around. A blanket of snow lay over everything.

"I feel like I'm walking in the clouds!" laughed Sparkle.

The twins started to explore.
"Look, Sparkle," called Silver.
"Berries!" He reached up to nibble
one, and nudged a branch. A dollop
of snow dropped onto his head!

"It looks like a hat," chuckled Sparkle.
Silver shook the snow off, sprinkling it everywhere.
"I can make it snow, too," he laughed.

Soon they came to a little clearing, at the top of
a gentle slope iced with snow. "Race you!" said
Silver, as he set off down the snowy hill. But his
feet skidded and slipped and –

whoosh!

"Be careful!" cried Sparkle. But by the time Silver
reached the bottom, he was laughing.
   "That was brilliant!" he said.
"I want to do it again!"

"Wait for me!" called Sparkle, and they slid down together, giggling all the way. It was so much fun, they did it again and again and again! They didn't notice that more snow was falling as they played.

At last, they started to feel tired. "I think it's time to go home," said Silver.

Sparkle looked around. "But which way is home?" she asked. "There's snow everywhere, and it all looks the same!"

"Don't be scared," said Silver bravely. "I think it's this way."

The little deer began to walk through the snow. It was very deep and it felt cold and heavy. They plodded on and on...

But after a while, they came back to the clearing.
"We're going round in circles!" cried Sparkle.
"We're lost!"

They looked around, wondering which way to go.
Then they saw a dark shadow coming towards them...

"Mommy!" the twins shouted happily. "We got lost!"
"You're safe now," said Mommy. "And we'll soon be home.
What do you think of the snow?"
"We had fun," said Silver. "But it's cold and a bit hard to
walk in," he added.

"You can follow in my footprints," said Mommy.
"It will be easier to walk that way."
So the twins set off, stepping safely in
Mommy's tracks.

Suddenly, they saw a strange shape. Silver and Sparkle jumped.

"Don't worry," laughed Mommy. "It's only a snowman. I think someone made him just for us — look what's in his basket."

"Carrots!" cried Silver, and they munched and crunched until just one carrot was left. It was the biggest carrot of all.

Silver reached up to take it, and – oops!
the snowman's hat slid onto Silver's head.

"Now you've got a real hat!" Sparkle laughed.
Silver smiled proudly. And when they reached home,
he shared the last carrot with Sparkle.

At bedtime, Silver and Sparkle
snuggled up with Mommy.
"I love snow," murmured Sparkle sleepily.
"I love snow too," said Mommy.
"Look how it sparkles like silver in the moonlight!"

The twins stared at each other in surprise.
"You gave us snow-names!" said Sparkle.
Mommy smiled and nodded,
"That's because I love snow…" she said.

"... and I love you."